IF SINGING WENT ON

by

GERALD CABLE

IF SINGING WENT ON

by

GERALD CABLE

Cirque Press
Copyright ©2024 Martha Farris

All rights reserved. No part of this publication may be reproduced, distributed or transmitted in any form or by any means, including photocopying, recording, or other electronic or mechanical methods, without the prior written permission of the publisher and author, except in the case of brief quotations embodied in critical reviews and certain other noncommercial uses permitted by copyright law.

Published by
Cirque Press

Sandra Kleven — Michael Burwell
3157 Bettles Bay Loop
Anchorage, AK 99515

Print ISBN:
978-1-7375104-9-9

cirquejournal@gmail.com
www.cirquejournal.com

Cover art by Tami Phelps, "Polychrome Pass"

Author photo by Suli Nee

Book Design by Signe Nichols

DEDICATION

Fairbanks, Alaska is a unique city, where the cold climate fosters close relationships, and new family lines are formed. It is the place where Jerry came of age, learned to craft his poetry and built a community of friends. This book is dedicated to that community, all of whom he loved and all who loved and supported him throughout his life. Specific thanks to Linda Schandelmeier for her support in finding a path to publication of these poems and to Paul Quist, the tallest tree in his forest of friends, for his guidance and support in the last chapter of Jerry's life.

ACKNOWLEDGMENTS

Abraxas, "Home Movie"
Ironwood, "Hellgrammite"
Shenandoah, "The Farm"
Nebraska Review, "After Dark," "Pine Grove Elementary"
Prairie Schooner, "Awake," "Someday"
Pennsylvania Review, "Trouble," "Axle"
Plainsong, "Conditions"
Carolina Quarterly, "To A Small Lizard," "Egg Lake"
Cimarron Review, "Counterweight"
Southern Poetry Review, "Mortality Tables"
South Coast Poetry Journal, "Pentecost"
Alaska Quarterly Review, "North Slope"
Cream City Review, "The Bees"
Connecticut Review, "One Morning," "Pioneer"
Another Chicago Magazine, "The Road to Cantwell"
Willow Springs, "Camp Job"
In the Dreamlight, "Ancient Forests of the Near East," "Mr. Pete Totten," "The Illumination of George Jr."
Permafrost, Vol. 2, #1, "The New Old Nenana Highway"
Permafrost, Vol. 2, #2, "Blue Clouds Over China," "To The East," "Internal Combustion"
Permafrost, Vol. 3, #2, "Fish," "Pine Grove Elementary"
Permafrost, Vol. 11, # 1, "Corona Box and Lumber," "Fish," "Mr. Pete Totten," "The Illumination of George Jr.," "Ancient Forests of the Near East," "The New Old Nenana Highway," "Thin Clouds," "Counterweight," "Pine Grove Elementary," "Under the House," "North Slope"

CONTENTS

I.

Harvest...15
Pine Grove Elementary...17
Domino...18
Starlight...19
Pentecost...20
In Blue Chalk...21
Mr. Pete Totten...22
Corona Box and Lumber...23
Driving Kay Santos Around Big Lake...24
Graduation...25
The Farm...26
The Boat...27
Counterweight...28
Egg Lake...30
The Embankment...32
Cutting Torch...34
The Illumination of George Jr. ...35
Union Hall...36
Home Movie...37

II.

Conditions...41
Fairbanks Exploration Co. ...43
The Open Cage...45
Hellgrammite...46
Monte Carlo Movement...47
Fish...48
Pioneer...49
Internal Combustion...50
Ancient Forests of the Near East...51
The Bees...52
For Martha...54

Speaking of the Weather...55
Something to Prove...56
New Museum of the North...57
Partners (American Creek, 1899)...59
The Road to Cantwell...61
Getting Away With The Truth...63
Falling in a Field...65
Blue Clouds Over China...66
Frost...67
North Slope...68
Under the House...70
The New Old Nenana Highway...72
December 10th...73
The Fields in Rain...74
Cold Windows...75
To a Small Lizard...76
Meditation...77
Camp Job...78
Kizhuyak Bay...79
Construction...80
After Dark...81
Looking for Martha...82
Surfacing...83
Yesterday Was Walt Whitman's Birthday...85
The Right Words...86
Battlefields Hit By a Rainstorm...87
Lower Camp...88
Lost...89
Red Handed at Thirty Below...90

III.

Awake...93
Decoy...94
The Deeps of Happiness...95
Third Grade...96
By the Pool...97
Because the Drum...98

Mortality Tables...99
Your Name in White...100
Overlooking the Airport...101
Sonnet to a More Tropical Saturday Afternoon...102
To The East...103
Axle...104
Trouble...105
From a True Story...106
Streamliner...107
Jet...108
Rivertrip...109
The Real Weather...110
One Morning...111
Refuse...112
It Moves, Soon It Will Fly...113
Terminal...114
Medicine...115
The Spring of '87...116
Ready or Not...117
Thin Clouds...118
Someday...119
Where...120
The Gamblers...121

About the Author...125
About Cirque Press...126
Books from Cirque Press...127
More Praise for *If Singing Went On*...129

I.

HARVEST

On the easy side of ecstasy,
I'm studying green waters for the wet, helpless nymphs
of crickets, scratching the bony back
of a half-tame egret with a bent-out coat hanger,
while my father and Mr. Rupe
are busy baling hay on the roof of the house.
The sun, its tiers of oars,
rows high, and they are threshing wheat
without wheels on the harvester.
The rafters have never been stronger.

Am I guilty, or disappointed?
Maybe he feels I'm not up to the strain of hard work,
not that I've delayed recovery,
the vertical incision
turning white,
a row with nothing in it.
Because now, it's also important to lie
easy in the cool floorboards
of the car, leaning
out over emerald water,
watching thick clumps of weed-root change
direction, no tide,
no current,
to inspect these floating islands for signs
of life, insects
at close range,
pretending, but not quite, the tithe
of pleasant obligations.

On the roof the baler shakes and clanks, rotates
its rhythmic jaw.
My father and Mr. Rupe bend,
blend into their work—pitchforks, wires, sacks
sweating from their straw hats
in a mist of yellow chaff:
Think how it itches down the neck, catches
in the throat....

Do I miss that feeling in my skin and eyes?
the structure of my body?

Everything is close.
Against the sky, on the low roof with my father,
the neighbor lends a hand for nothing.
Except for his thin wife,
still beautiful in her round glasses,
there is nothing
he loves more.
Singing with a soft accent,
his large hands hold, bury deep as he guides
the plow into sleep.

The green water is full of life,
things are moving just beneath the surface.
The egret is helping itself.

PINE GROVE ELEMENTARY

Broken in the center where it thins
along her name
I hold the stone with sticks and raise
the rotted palings of a fence,
brittle wire I have to
tear from the grasp of weeds.
She died in childbirth—the words, cut deep
in 1875, are slow in healing.

Back of the schoolyard, where trees begin,
she gathers what's left: the sky
when we're through
on a green, splintery swing, one room
for school. While
the first bird killed by the smoke house sings
in the spent shell
something else I don't know how to love

begins to break on its own.
A thick, green splinter in my arm, all afternoon
the chalk dust floating through my hair.
In sunlight the bottomless pond
at the foot of the hill turns blue,
caught out at night
her stillborn darkness tears at my skin,
my thin wheels spin gravel.

I sleep to a light wedged in the door.
At her side a yellow pine out circles my arms,
the hollow fills with needles
and snow.

Last year I drove through and the road
was paved, there's a strong,
white fence, and slow, the stone cemented,
her first name, Susanna.

DOMINO

Like my father, I was in
between wars—though they turned
the boat around
beginning the last one:
The troop ship Mann, squeaking
by Asia on a dumb line for San
Francisco. My duties would have been to die
in my earphones
like ice tongs, in the back
of a truck.
What I did do was nothing, top
secret in the tertiary alleys
of Naha.
When I missed a training film,
and the sergeant
acting tough,
like a thin fish turned sideways, his elbows
akimbo, asked
Why! I said I didn't
feel like it: neither wise nor unknowing.
So, though he chewed my ass
in a military manner,
he had no teeth in his heart. But then
way up high, barking
down their chains of command,
they did,
and the heads began to roll.

STARLIGHT

He lived up the road, we were kids
in a small country, no pasta
or tennis.
I trusted Bill's driving.
Following him home over ten-thousand
nights ago
in a rattletrap pick-up, dead

short in the headlights,
going by his, red
glow at his bumper like a candle
flickering in the dust...
about a mile a minute,
he killed his lights, flipped
everything off.

I remember no moon, not
a sliver, frozen
to the wheel. He had
bushy eyebrows
and his ears stuck out.
I never knew what he was doing.
But you couldn't touch

the brake, change
anything, the dark
exploding through the windshield,
    One life later,
I went by the tips
of the telephone poles, barely
standing out

in the starlight.

PENTECOST

Late forties, in the drizzling shade
of walnut trees
and an inch of dust,
cars are parked
around the tent of revelations.
We sit on wooden benches
facing the platform where my grandmother drives
the holy spirit
into the keys of a scarred piano.
Also up there, standing out at the edge
of the boards, thin
for his suit, a man with a buzzing
guitar, whose eyes
shine up through the canvas.
Everyone sings,
and the singing lifts, my grandmother
highest—until seems
the blinding Holy Ghost might spring
from the tight spiral
of her white hair. Suddenly a large

woman looms up, rolling
her head, fluttering eyes, her tongue
unleashed from the world
into the clear words of her soul
in its pale, blue dress.
And waving her hands, terror
and jubilation flying from her fingers,
she rises
over ironing boards, dishes
stacked in the sink,
and the white
crisco melting in a black, iron pan.

IN BLUE CHALK

Culling sheep years ago, a day
in the dust of their hooves, he drew the X
on Leroy's back, who was out
of the know, unwiring the wrong gates,
a gap in his smile. Now hooked
on a barstool, backfired joke in his face,
he's the one weak in the shoulders.
Where we laughed before,
nothing is funny—living next door
to the bar
in a fleabitten room, sheep
lost, sold down the river. He's out
of his life.
When Leroy took off his jacket that night,
saw he'd been branded
to be skinned
for his two dollar hide,
he must've felt stabbed in the throat:
Something he'd known all along, forgotten
again. The other,
who'd written the cross, good
in his teeth, bright eye
of the day,
now wears it under his shirt, down
through his skin
on the blade of his heart.

MR. PETE TOTTEN

Grey stubble, a wise-crack light
in his eyes, we rode
a hard-
sprung candy wagon
on washboard roads at 5 a.m.
The clang
of his gorgeous hangover.
Then, at noon
we were following the last
log we'd chokered
down a steep skid trail to the landing,
when a chewed-up sapling
bent flat underneath sprang up
and smote Pete
just under the brim
of his hardhat,
right between his
Irish eyes. Had his skull
been a bronze bell
the fallers up in the tall timber
would have laid aside
their chainsaws, listening.
I watched him kneel
in the dusty needles—already
having nursed in his hands all morning
the deep, tight
wedge in his brow.
Standing, slow, the light was blurred
in his eyes. Whatever
I felt, was not pain
in my young, smooth face
and I sprang onto a stump, freshly cut,
yellow as the sun,
the wide rings for good years,
reveling in my ignorance.

CORONA BOX AND LUMBER

High in his armchair of levers, Swan
minutely tunes the lathe's
hydraulic knives,
his pale, blue-veined hands aligning
to the finest knots
in whirling logs of yellow pine,
slicing into long sheets, maps of sunlight
on the cutting belt; pulls the chucks
and lets them drop
like bones.

My job, with a blistering pike that breaks
its bite
so I stumble back into metal walls; drag
the sap-heavy cores, stack
and bind them square and tight, oozing
in steel straps
for the whining forklift.
Meanwhile, Swan

in thick, glinting glasses,
as though studying the limb of the sky
shining through the kilns,
flicks the levers six ways at once, things
imagined, a pilot flying in…
and the green heartwood piles
to the blades.

A long, sharp whistle to quit by
but my muscles, in the shoulder of July
swamp-cooler drizzling
on the roof, stay knotted all night.
Swan, I dream, carries

his lunchbox full of feathers.

DRIVING AROUND BIG LAKE WITH KAY SANTOS

I let her drive
the two-tone Olds, desert-something-
cream, four door
family car.
Her smooth, dark skin.
And she loses track, fades
on a gentle curve,
Smirnoff in her fledgling blood
and mine.

But one eye watched—
feeling in my bones
the afterthought of spattered glass,
that steep wall of boulders
rising from the dark
invisible lake—
and I wrenched the wheel
away, we spun
to the opposite ditch
springing the hood
as we hit.

Tires squalled from the rim,
and I walked about
light-headed, testing
my knees.
That Sunday, my father drove out
and inspected the tread-marks
that ran along for a hundred feet
on the edge.
Close, he said,
forgetting the crease
in the hood.

GRADUATION

As if practiced, I reached out
with the wrong
right hand. I got it anyway,
having learned to judge
a stereo, string up a fence, forget
history. We wanted
our names in paint (the sheriff
saw them there)
on the silver tank overlooking town, that
we had to repaint, scraping
the dripping, red
obscenities, genitals
named for a teacher: Faintly,
even today, in certain
light, if you look
just right…
Someone got sand in their eyes
and couldn't fight.
We slugged beer on into the night.
Where were we supposed to go
in our see-through shirts
to get rid of ourselves
while the moon
rained milk on bales of alfalfa
scattered in the fields
like small coffins.

THE FARM

The car left melting in sunlight,
I climb a barbed-wire fence into a field of rock
and sparse, pale grass,
walk, as pacing a distance, toward the farm,
its grove of tall poplars shining
at the foot of a barren ridge.

Once, a house of tall ceilings,
long, screened-in porch, an attic whose windows
faced due south, until the nails
gave way and walls, rafters,
the tin-roof for counting rain
spilled down in a blossom of dust swept quickly away
in the broad, east wind.

A place of cracked plows sheathed in rust.
They'd hacked at the ground, buried
the seeds. Snow mixed with starlight crumpled the barn,
the smoke house on its side
like a coffin heaved from the earth.

But the orchard, the gnarled
limbs of its trees cracked and broken,
goes on working,
turning out small, yellow fruit
for a hundred birds. And when the cool skin

of an apple they've missed breaks in my teeth,
under the sweetness
a wild flavor wells up, remote
as the sky. Foundations opened to the sun, an end
that endures, growing bitter milkweed
where the floor was.

THE BOAT

My uncle, who once fixed Mickey
Rooney's furnace and whose back was zippered
with scars—he saved
his kidney stones in jars—owned
the boat with the bad,
round bottom,
and aluminum. Out on the river my father
was the one who stood up, playing
a rainbow, spilling it over.
My aunt came up under
the boat,
thinking the sun had gone down.
Like their tackle and beer: straight
to the bottom
And the river was deep and wet
and put out my father's cigar. Maybe
a few plugs and bobbers floated up,
and they saved one pole—
the lucky one
with the fish on.

COUNTERWEIGHT

He leans through a canvas curtain
to grasp you
beneath the jaw, bending
your neck by the soft, unrelenting edge
of his strength.
Slung to a wide leather strap
at his chest
the rope passing through a single pulley
the counterweight
rises and sinks.
Although your handsome eyes
like polished burls
of maple
roll white, he sits you quickly adrift
on your spine, in the clasp
of his knees—and begins
at your throat. The greasy clouds
that lent you a cool
rounded-off feeling
are shorn away, rippling your skin
revealing the warm
pink sky of your belly. Each tuft
the hollows
behind your ears, the pockets
of your thighs, undone
to the shining floor, gathered in twine
and trampled together
into long sacks of burlap that are sewn
shut and hauled away.
Through a second curtain, bleeding
or not, you are shoved
into a narrow pen with the others
your head now heavy,
held low, the ears protruding.
These are the flat-lands, steel towers
wavering in the heat
the chirring of the cutters

in the long, red barn. You shiver flies
and blink
in the hard, white sun.

EGG LAKE

A long time since water,
and nothing grows where we walk
its bed of alkali dust
looking for arrowheads, a spearpoint
if we're lucky,
washed out in the last rain. Poking sticks
into what seem like pockets
of powdered bone
for the glint of black glass—we find
pieces, one
nearly perfect—the tip
broken off—shaped like a tiny heart,
for birds. Later,
starting back into the low slant
of September, needles
are falling from the trees
around the shoreline. Nick,

his glasses switching light like signals mirrored
to someone in the mountains,
will take his death this year and leave.
Nell will give me arrowheads,
each one remembered by where it was found.
Long-distance, her voice
grown brittle,
not afraid to say she's lonely.
No longer looking
through Modoc county and into Nevada
for what someone made
who had a name, chipping
from a mountain of glass when the lake was a body
of water.

Shaft and feathers, the one who tightly
wrapped the sinew
that held them together,
lost on a shimmering surface of white dust.

Finding the shape of what has lasted,
calling to the others,
"found one!" Feeling ahead,
touching hands through obsidian.

THE EMBANKMENT

The road winds steeply down,
through lava beds, stray fields of manzanita,
leaves gleaming in the early heat
of July; crosses
a cattle guard, clanking as we pass, enters
a cool oasis: shade trees, sprinklers
on the lawn, and ends up
at the power house, set deep in bedrock,
tall windows ajar.

Sizzling wires droop across a swimming pool
filed with shafts
of dusty light.
In the spillway, water boils up like the fear
of falling in. We grip a railing
that trembles with the dynamos
that do our thinking for us. Back

on the highway that follows the canyon rim, we stop
at an overlook— handbrake
tight. Fresh tire-tracks land off the edge
as if they might
continue on, a mile across, it seems
on the other side
among the jackrabbits and parched juniper.
Leaning out,
peering down between sheer walls, traces

of an earlier boulder-strewn,
obliterated by slides of shale...
And the river.
Upstream, near the falls, mist rising
like white dust, that seem to roar
in field glasses, a bridge
an arc of rusting steel, its roadway of planks
rotted and broken through.
Then we lose

that twisting road beneath us. Or, down there,
we've lost the one above:
Now we face a long, hard climb, grasping
at roots and crevices,
back to where we thought we stood, sun
light on our backs, rising
higher, above a farther, skyward embankment
of loose, red cinders.

CUTTING TORCH

Measured by eye, the work is sketched in chalk.
Opening brass valves
he strikes a flame, tunes it
to a deft, blue knife.
Lowers his glasses. His body

bends into smoke, showers of sparks, slag
cooling at his shoes as one hand
steadies the other, urging
the dry whistle
of fire

around—A rind of steel clatters to the floor.
Stepping back, he shows the inside
glowing red and sparking
edges, heat-colors
like dark rainbows, vitriol

mixed with soot. Blossoms. Seized, weighing
what it does, in easy tongs, plunged
into the cold Ohio.
A white plume rises
from the river, breathing out.

His word is strong.

THE ILLUMINATION OF GEORGE JR.

He lost it one night
on that long stretch between Canby and Adin,
Adin spelled out in white rocks
on the hillside. Can of beer
cooling his thighs,
bullet-nosed forty-nine Ford

the easy drift of eighty-five
striped world
running beneath while he dozed
at the spoke of the wheel—Woke
in a blizzard of sparks
the smell and steady grind of burnt maroon
as this, our good car of no wars
flipped to its roof, skimmed the asphalt
and rolled over five times
out through the starry jack pines.

Perfect letters tilted
at the sky
high on the barren slope behind the town.
Three streets lined in shade trees,
and a cold,
brown river. Its dying hitch-hiker

several years gone
when I saw George
on the third day, moving lightly
from the door of his father's
grease-pit garage,
softly among the blessings
of gutted mufflers, the worn-out prayers
of bald tires—
in the quick new flower of his skin.

UNION HALL

I dream my father
dead and missing for twenty years,
the star-point of his badge
shot from the stone,
my father goes down
with me to the union hall
where I owe money in back dues—
he shows me the note
from the steward, gilt-edged
as if from an angel.

The morning hour
too early
and I'm reluctant, as usual,
to walk through that hall of white smoke
where men are slumped,
dealing out hands
of hearts,
to walk beside my father who blazes
inside, who is slowly,
and with pride
growing younger than I.

HOME MOVIE

Beyond a white murkiness, like erasures
in the blue sky,
everything is clear.
He is wearing a hat
of finely woven straw, the gold wire
of his glasses
shines, and the tree
guards him like a green fire.

This quick spool of film, its edges spiked
by the bright sun
of 1960, is the last scene
of my father's life. All the snapshots
from the 30's, on motorcycles
with his cap pushed back,
or later, holding up stringers
of white-bellied trout,

cigar-stub gracing one side
of his mouth, lead
to this hand-held July
where the barn
and the steep-
roofed smokehouse still stand, where he steps
from the porch
passing through the pure, black

shade of a poplar,
toward the tall, red mare, white blaze
on her chest, always
hungry, shoving at the fence.
He feeds her an apple from his palm
ignoring all around him
the blur
and the chattering sprockets,

strokes her soft, blind nose—turns
to see us

where we watch in the firing lens
of my sister's camera, and waves, once
showing a fine touch
by the hand
a gesture of both greeting
and farewell.

II.

CONDITIONS

The sun shines in the windows and I'm sailing
out to help myself, and if becalmed
I'll row with my hands, gathering the red
and yellow roses of horizons
in my arms, and the grey hills.
And if all the doors in all the blue houses
were held open
I would not return.

They do not send back to tell us how they fare.
Leaving hard knots in the strings
of sleep only the small
skilled fingers of dreams
can loosen. You find the lost mine
out in the hills, its rusted shovels and mattocks,
their handles perished,
or the empty ship
with coffee brewing in the galley. Suddenly (that other
shoe), after a long day beneath the "don't worry"
of scattered clouds
a rock will crack the windshield.

I'll meet you there at eight o'clock,
and if there's no money for wine,
we'll bring good weather
and call it even.
Regret can have the bones, the only thing
that's true that isn't is the loss of difference
dissolved into a hundred years
and the imperfect face
that blossomed in yesterday's clouds.

Ah! rain on the roof. Sentimental
over pencilled names in the cover of a family Bible,
scrawled as if written
on a bad road. I feel watched by the darkness

in a cardboard box at the end
of the driveway. A single depth-charge eye. A rock

has cracked the windshield, a web,
slivers of glass.
Until it seems there are traces of wind
in the roots of trees
where our clothes have been hung to dry, their pockets
gathered full of light.
We lose ourselves in a glance, and we vanish
from each other's arms,
a gesture on the crest of a hill, a green wave.

FAIRBANKS EXPLORATION CO.

1.
Zones of rusted metal grown flimsy
with mare's tail, fireweed
in the ditches, the spewed, conical hills
of tailings, a boiler,
the gut of a locomotive
for steam-points to melt auriferous gravel,
its black veins perishing,
heavy door
cast open, cold ashes in the grate
and a yellowjacket's nest
depending on its
fragile stem
of mud.
Steam-rollered pythons
are tangles of conveyor belts weathered
into yellowing swirls
and stripes,
machinery in thickets of alder
in moonlight soft
as petals
though to lay a hand on the teeth
of their massive gears
is like dropping a slug in the heart.
Ravens in the skull
of an ore-shaker, hunched
on its four tracks, each
with a powerful, dead motor.
Then the greatest dragline dinosaur
in the Northwest,
Bucyrus Erie, boom laid out
on blocks, where ants
protect their pale eggs,
The solid jaw of its bucket cast off
with a drink of meltwater
and pebbles to eat,

and at the end of the healing road
the dredge, extinct
mechanical swan, moored
in the center of the lake it gouged,
a loon swimming back
and forth in its steel-
shuttered reflection riding ripples
of moonlight.

2.
Twenty years ago the dredge master
threw back the levers
and shut down
Dredge #12—Hungarian riffles,
trommel screen, rolling
quicksilver, sluices and the gold-saving tables
scraped clean.
The steel masts turn white
with bird droppings,
but standing tonight in the shadow of a spoke
of the great drive-wheel
I hear a step
in the broken glass above me.

THE OPEN CAGE

An open cage of driftwood
and dry nettles

while the birch trees
slowly lean (Triassic
to Jurassic)
to the ground and
the spruce
with their green eyes begin to reign
and that also is not
the end

the clouds
the snow

the ruts in the road

my presence arriving on the glass

outside the birds
one another
circling

HELLGRAMMITE

Clouds drift
through the stream of his flesh
and the swirl of wild color in my side
wells up in his eyes. Drift
down in the ink
pouring out from the grass
at his feet. Lunge!
swallow this six-legged worm of a fly,
its steel spine—
The filament snaps taut
like a nerve,
the barb biting hard in my gut,
and I wake to the raw
cutting edge of my lips.

I outweigh his heart,
I know the dreams he's spent on air,
that he swims behind breath.
And I leap
in the twisting light, strive
to catch him back through that last small eye
at the tip of his life, shorn of clothes,
the watch stripped from his wrist
ticking at the sharp
green edge of the sun.
His hat,
red fly in its brim.

I cannot cry.
Draw him down, mouth
into mine, deep until his breath unwinds
the hooks in my ribs
and we swim.

MONTE CARLO MOVEMENT*

Sheiks arrive in private jets,
while the rest of us, born every minute,
have coffee in Barstow
and drive the hard glare
past Windmill Station, Highway 15.

The Stardust rakes in millions,
and the hustler
in an oxblood shirt lies
in wait at the light between casinos,
offering a deal.

You could drive up to Indian Springs
or down to Searchlight,
Nevada, but you'll never make Utah: poking
little holes in the clouds,
white scars

of condensation. And while the light
of this last resort is arriving,
you stroll the Botanical Gardens
near Tucson, with a sweetheart, the best part
of yourself, jingling

what's left in your pockets
and observing a mouse who lives
without water, who takes the cactus sun
for granted,
the cruel stars as well.

The MX missile shell game

FISH

The ocean floor is littered with the conical
teeth of sharks. A pickerel,
its lower jaw protruding, is fierce.
If facts could breathe in, in their sleep,
go nowhere, an airline ticket to last August
found in a musty pocket of your suitcase
(tin of aspirin, the loose change) you'd lie
and say nothing, or as water
boils for a ninth cup of tea and a stone
dropped in the river will not fly east
or even swim upstream, say
that things are different now—as in the instance

of moonlit smoke that rolls from the stovepipe,
its shadow pouring uphill
across a fathom of melting snow.

    Like any sailor
saves his fingers, you squeeze out the flavor
by simply placing a teabag in a spoon
and winding the string around. When you walk

into this day with a steaming cup, afraid to
burn your lip, the fish (the coelacanth
is another one) understand
by the feel of footsteps in the water. You waver,
a loosened pebble blinks once
and they swim away to find you.

PIONEER

Like a tinfoil hat to celebrate the end
spin-flipped into sky
after sky
their raw, separate outlines tattooed
on its anodized skin.
No tree, flower

but his genitals, as if the carriers
of fire-root and berry
tapped to the dark
inner belly. Her breasts
grow dim
with interstellar dust

as with her hands open on her thighs
she gives, insensibly
the frequency of hydrogen.
And where into the warped
fabric of darkness do they travel,

tossed from one shore of strewn glass
to another,
getting nowhere,
a map of fourteen pulsing stars
against their backs?
To someone with the kind of eye

that can decipher
and bring them back, a wish
for more than our common survival?
And when they arrive
the thin ghosts of Martians are tilling
the glitter

the fragments of leaves.

INTERNAL COMBUSTION

Yesterday at the R & S
Machine shop
a twisted crankshaft
journals shined with oil.
Laid out on a dolly

the cylinder heads with four
or six vestigial eyes
were propped on the benches
in a torqueless stupor

and the engine blocks with six
or eight deep thoughts going nowhere
without their lovely pistons
could only stare into the corrugated sky

where metal dust
drifted up
to glint in a perfect bar of sunlight.

ANCIENT FORESTS OF THE NEAR EAST

Straighten up, almost broke
my back—but I've flattened the springs
of a two-ton truck
with log-ends. It was only last night
while the moon, her bones
poking through, held sway in a wild corner
of the sky
and the stars
threw down their cards, that a fine chill
touched at the roots of my neck.

This year, no scavenging hip-deep
in dead-white snow for twigs
and scraps of lumber crusted over
with icy leaves.
Right outside that window, which
that moth will never fathom—tiers
of wood
stacked in long rows. Soon the stovepipe
in blossom across the forests of Mohenjo-daro.

THE BEES

Cloudy and cool,
they must have thought summer was over
too soon, and there I was
with a can of smoldering rags, counting
their honey.
Like a rainstorm starting down
in one drop, she flew up
buzzing my face, that white,
moist planet looming in their midst.
And with her sting in my lip, dangling
her thread of gut,
I backed away, pawing at the air, turned
and ran in the house, slammed the door, panic
like pollen sticking to my skin. But the madness
still buzzed in my ear
 and the stinging, hot needles
so I ran again, out the back
breaking through where weeds gripped
the gate, into trees and alder like whips
but I never slowed, my footprints still ringing the water
I hit
when I was gone.

    At last,
I came to a place that seemed right, a kind
of meadow, a glade the sun
never missed, neither dim
nor too bright, warm and peaceful.
So I shook the bees
from my hair
and all day they went from flower to flower
and in the evening they came to me and danced
in my eyes, and I began learning
the dance, its strength,
discovery, surprise,
and its music, whose open notes sang clear and close
as the sky in its darkness,

though the source seemed
far, distant as the starlight.

FOR MARTHA

Shoveling in last year's garden
we strike upon a blank Rosetta Stone,
and clearing the dirt, pry it loose
from the cool shape
of its bed
exactly as if it were molded there
in utter darkness
then flooded with sunlight.
Digging our heels into the soft furrows
we tip it up
into the wheelbarrow, wobble
down to the house, between the trees—
a foothold for the doorway.

There is rain
and snow, the sun trades off
with a worn-thin moon,
we lose the heart between us, unknown
as hieroglyphics of birds,
serpents, a man with a sail…
until we kneel closer,
and then the words appear like stars
and though many are broken
at the edges
they shine
and spark translation.

SPEAKING OF THE WEATHER

Remember that summer near Fairbanks, the rain
fell like someone
on the radio crumpling cellophane
while the birch trees lashed
at the windows, their leaves
a green blindness,
while Siberia sweltered?

A cold, driving rain in July, unusual
for the Interior, so that the sun
was a grey blur
and the garden would not move.
Only the strawberries shone red
through visqueen
and chickweed thrived without chickens.

Raining on into August and September
like the hiss recorded
around the voice of Woodrow Wilson,
and I dug out
a gag of the last generation,
that bright-orange, vacuum-sealed can
of "California Sunshine."

Clear and 95 in Kolyma:
the patterns were stable and the driveway
washed out. Inside the windows,
the walls were streaked and flowing
with clear-shadowed veins of rainwater,
crossing our hands and faces
as if they were real.

SOMETHING TO PROVE

Leave your knives in the tray
and step through the metal detector,
trying not to see
the ghostly grenades x-rayed
in your carry-on luggage.
Board the flight to L.A., buckle, smoke
when the no smoking is gone.
Arrive. Visit a cousin who thinks you steal
an old family watch. Catch the bus
to Louisville via Reno-Salt Lake, hear a boxing
match in your fillings. Arrive, check your fly, rent
a car from one of the girls, eat
a toasted cheese, laugh and sip weak, burning
coffee between bites.
Wear good clothes and try to walk
upright. Lose
a dime in a broken phone booth. Fill out
three applications, then
tie your shoes.
Take a long, long walk, have cocktails, fall
in love and find your way home
to your room; remember
the number?
Use the key, flush the toilet, tv.
Raise the blind and look
out the window.
Write her name,
touch your lips
with the pencil
eraser, and the
taste of metal,
lie down, dream
you fell asleep
with the light on.

NEW MUSEUM OF THE NORTH

Nine feet in dead air,
shotgun nostrils,
the sky of his face
snapped off
in the middle of a day, Great Kodiak
tilted out
as if peering down this blue, shining hallway
for a bus, earth-ripping
claws hooked at his side, ready to dig
for small change
while dry leaves drift over bones of salmon
in the hole behind his eyes.

Ice begins to lift, cracking the rivers,
the grass turns pale green.
Farther back
in the dusk, still working out
in its huge skull
the meaning of survival, the buffalo
turns to face
a blizzard in the wall
where the long, curved tusks of mastodons
are leaning. Music
filters softly
from the ceiling. Shading my eyes

I squint through the grating.
I've delivered the wildflowers pressed
in newspaper
and today we are moving the boats
of brittle skin,
the birdfeather vest from nineteen-ten.

Soon a strong light
will be switched on for the grand opening—

a sudden glare, the seal
poised to dive
from her plywood-spit of gravel, held tight
in the clasp of her bones.

PARTNERS (AMERICAN CREEK, 1899)

At dusk, while the sweat cooled out
in their clothes
and the coffee grounds settled,
they rolled cigarettes, twisted the ends
talking fine, Frisco women
and rounds for the house.
They raised this sod-roof cabin,
flour-sack curtain
unfurled in the window—
then bent to the rocks with shovels
and mattocks
and the gold trickled out. But slowly

rose an old resentment, then the quarrel
like grease
spitting in the pan—
and a line was drawn
to split the room
and the last word was spoken,
only blunt notes
with a pencil stub between them.
At supper they rolled down
their sleeves,
buttoned them up
and scraped the blue, metal plates

in silence,
while the lantern sipped
and fluttered
its soft, yellow wings at the walls.
Six months while the sluice-box
was humming
they cracked their spines in the rocks,
sleeping each night
in blisters of dream light
as if they could not breathe

the same air.
Slowly they funneled

the dust into long leather bags.
Near the end of autumn,
as the century rolled off
on its iron wheel,
they weighed to the grain
and left,
each without looking back, three days
apart. Rain and snow
aimed down the stovepipe
and the stove rusted out. Now,
new light
seeps through the logs

and fireweed blooms on the roof.

THE ROAD TO CANTWELL

In the early morning hours of August
the northern light begins
to mix with dark
and you can no longer see between the days.
Driving the steep curves above
Ester Creek, I see her
in time—dead-on
to my wheels
and swerve, with my heart
cold, white. And when
I turn back—the moon pours
through the birch leaves,
shimmers on the powerlines—
she is leaning to her good arm, resting
from her long climb
on the wrong road to Cantwell.
She sits in the center, escaping
mosquitoes who love her
and sing their wings
in the wayside brush. Old woman
who lives, she says,
on the Colville River, in a village
north of roads,
wears a cast on her wrist
and carries belongings
in a net sack
for oranges.
The road she needs

meets this one at the foot of the hill.
She looks for money, will pay
if I'll take her to Cantwell,
miles, too far to drive. Here
on this long black river
I'll leave you. Take these cigarettes,
keep to the edge

under that single streetlamp
bending its neck to the gravel,
and follow the road,
how it veers to the south.

Cantwell is there.

GETTING AWAY WITH THE TRUTH

It's the dogs that don't wake us
when we sleep.
A friend of a friend, his father
shooting through the floor
at the gnawing that kept him awake.
A few days later,
this second-hand friend down on his hands
and knees with the spiders—teeth
grinning white
in the webs: dead
rat perfume in the crawl-space.
Spiders don't keep us awake,

they keep to themselves, their looms
like unbearable music—unless
we build one up
in a dream, one leg at a time—fear
of a fear—and then too many.
It could be a dream
in the news: reaching for a jar
in the cellar, one jumps
in her mouth, lands
on her tongue, hourglass glowing
with venom. Everything
we didn't say,
or did because we hadn't.
Strapped in the ambulance, breathing
hard through the swelling.

But the dogs,
the dogs woke us up
once, when the door came open
in the stove
and a sparkling log rolled out of the smoke.

We took them outside
for a roll in the snow
and we howled at the moon,
telling it all.

FALLING IN A FIELD

Along the road
to the experimental farm
long rows in sheets of plastic
to the dry spruce
on one side, the white
birch on another—and the hill cutting off
from the sky
a moment of light.

Mid-afternoon, the pungent spice of spring,
driving at our ease,
while out in the sky an airplane
throttles down—
a figure tumbles out
into open air
plummets for an instant—
until the chute blossoms in panels of red
and blue. We watch
as the faller twists his body, tugs
and spills the breath,

an urgency of motion
that catches us, watching now from the roadside
gripping our throats
around the vacuum of his falling—
the world rising up
in changing planes of pattern
as he glides himself from roads,
powerlines
to the center of the field
where he crumples in the furrows, stands
and gathers in the shrouds.

BLUE CLOUDS OVER CHINA

for William Stafford

The man from California is on the verge
of being wrong,
he pours a glass of sand.
Another, living inland, among all those borders
of being right, was only
nice—he seemed to love, exactly,
the backs of his hands, their rumors
of blood and spokes of bone.
Or perhaps, as he turned one hand, opened
to give us someone's name, he felt the knuckles
subside into his fingers
then rise ten moons on an open sea.

Nice.
But other wrongs begin to lose their rights.
An ocean tastes the long cracked rib of California
where it may not rain for years—trout
will drown in sunlight—or fall
at once all week until these rainbows
swim the rafters.
I see what I'm about to say, I love
the truth of weather
exploding through the nicest day a wind
that's hard and mean
that clears the sky into a still blue passenger.

FROST

Hands sharpened in the leaf,
her face awry in the cool, garden light.
She pulls the vines of good tomatoes, green bells
across her shoulder, leaves the ones
that spoiled
where they touched the ground.

The sheltering rhubarb, its pale, red stem,

the trees grown high
and white potatoes spill from her arms.

More weeds, tough, thick, and everything
tangled in their roots—

Saving what's left

she has driven here on the steep hill, stopped
in familiar ruts,
peered into the sheet-metal mirror that leans
on the woodpile, flowers
dying on the steps, yellow and red.

Almost dark.

Rasp of cucumbers, the blank face
of the moon.
Saving what's left, everything, the fragile leaves,
the cold heart of joy.

NORTH SLOPE

At Franklin Bluffs a strong light
burns in the curtains.
I walk out from the camp and its revved-up
generators, to an abandoned
airstrip, glad for the brisk wind grounding mosquitoes.

Two caribou, still pale, skittish,
surprised by the vast, sudden greenness
of the tundra, watch me
in a moment of such open intensity
I might only drop to my hands
in reply. The bluffs

rise along the river (someone who once
lifted me high),
the one relief on this smooth slant
of the world—except for pingos:
small knolls for squirrels and flowers,
nowhere to spend my money.

In the center of a small lake, five loons
are swimming,
their indelible colors absorbed
in the sheen—the sun
still burning past midnight, gathering up

spreading them out on the northern horizon,
squaring them off
into blocks, until they seem like huge,
shimmering cities.
The wind dropping for an instant:
mosquitoes swarm up in my face.

The bluffs are tinted rose, a metropolis
without windows rises
from the Arctic Ocean and the blinding

sun still burns the day
when my grandfather, who never talked
behind anyone's back, died

at the Red Bluff Roundup. I still
can't get it straight
where he went, and all my old prayers
into death
settle back on my skin, like snow
from this solid, blue sky.

A truck leaves scarlet clouds.
I walk to the crossroads where a riverweight,
ten-thousand pounds of concrete
with "Sitka" boldly written
in black paint
on the northern-facing side, leans

into the ancient gravel.
The airstrip is crumbling,
the windsock fades from something bright,
tattered on its hinge,
still holding invisibly true
to the long breathing out of the wind.

UNDER THE HOUSE

Was it the stove-pipe crimpers, lost
in another shuffle?
I've forgotten. A carburetor for the Skylark
whose body was compressed
between hydraulic jaws
into a solid book of metal,
like my skull when the passenger's gone—
only turned inside—
fragments of blue paint from dreams
of flying
clinging to the inner surface.

No longer aware of the rain
that's fallen since morning, moving
half-crouched, shaking a flashlight;
a spider has spun its web
in the cracked chimney of a lantern,
in a mildewed box, beneath
an ancient toaster
a small round can with stars
and ringed planets on its lids—
<u>Carter's Midnight Typewriter Ribbon.</u>
Prying the rusted lip

listening inside, the jingle like coins,
I think I've found mementos,
the winter trip to Europe—dimes
of the Netherlands
too tiny to spend. Shining
down the light
to see what I've saved
for the afterworld: galvanized buttons
and a safety pin.
Deeper in the box, shrews
have eaten through the cardboard

leaving their black seeds.
And gouged records from the flood

I'd love to sail out
upon the Arctic Ocean, among the gulls.
Outside, the hush of rain.
I fasten my sleeve with the pin—
there's nowhere to step, the eyes
of spiders
are sprinkled everywhere
out over the dark hills, the cool graves
without a blade of grass.

THE NEW OLD NENANA HIGHWAY

I wind myself up
the hill on a slow bicycle
one eye on the roadside
for something lost
between the beer cans
with their sip of rusty
rainwater.

Somewhere there's fire
and smoke
seeps in along the valleys.

Finding the top
I stop for my knotted leg
a dandelion flares up in the ditch
burning yellow
and a rabbit shies back
into green,
impassable alder.

This year the road crew
of the highways is cutting it back
from the windshields
and in the seventh year
rabbits thump under tires
and the pavement is stained
with indecision.

Blurring in the spokes it was
of no importance. I glide
for a moment

Disappear into a curve.

DECEMBER 10TH

On her birthday the wind
is gusting out of the east, and upstairs
all those windows lose
their nine times share of the heat.
It costs to see.

See my reflection among Christmas lights
Martha has strung around
two of the windows that jut out
like the prow of an ark anchored
here in the side of this hill.

A neighbor has a tall spruce plugged in
with all the colors bright
in a darkness still pure at eight
in the morning. The distant lights of town,
we know they do not celebrate so much.

There is only a scattered snow that falls,
but the wind drifts over the driveway—
I may have to call the plow.
It is dark, Emily, cold, and the world sails hard for the sun.

THE FIELDS IN RAIN

Before the wind dies
down it brings rain, undoing
pebbles along the river banks, rocks
and boulders break loose, rolling
into white-water ravines, leaving
in their places smooth sockets in the earth.
Dust
is washed from the leaves of nettles,
the wet fields roll like smoke
and shine within themselves

And as I start across these fields
my shoes grow heavier,
larger with every step
until, mired to the shins, twisting my body
like a glued dancer afraid
to fall, one
is lost,
the raw earth giving birth to a cold,
naked foot. Then, it no longer
matters, the other

is lost too.

COLD WINDOWS

For the brittle fish whose eyes
are glass,
the changed water
is white, salt, breath on the cold window
between us. Only buttons
saved like bones, awls
in burlap bags. December,

the river frozen solid in its bed, anchored
in its bay of silt. Fish
held fast. Gather up
and carry out
smoking griefs, my little crimes
igniting candles
of mere misgiving.

And digging through what snow the wind
has left, leave
these worn-smooth things, such
as feelings, like souvenirs, lucky charms
intended for no one
but you, my tongue—and heart—
and toothless soul.

TO A SMALL LIZARD

When the pressure ridge gives way, peaches
fall from trees
bruising themselves on California.
She rings from an enclave of windows over-
looking the fault.
Awake, still breathing

water, words slip
into the wires, rattle the little green dish
in the earpiece.
Needles leap
at who we are, discontinuity,
the scar

half-hidden in the part of my hair—all
scaled down to a small
translucent lizard she'd seen that afternoon
in the library, seeming
pure solid

but when it moved everything
moved at once.

MEDITATION

A man idles by in a pickup only
so shiningly red, apart
from the sun, because the snow,
because of the red
truck, is whiter than snow.
Beside him a black dog, alertly
taking in light.
The man, by the way
he appears, the tilt
of his head, is relaxed,
feeling good in this smooth truck whose red paint
paints the sky blue
on the hood,
moving down the white street on round,
black tires,
bringing the dog,
his own hands beyond him, out of reach
far off
at the wheel.

CAMP JOB

Spent the day in the tunnel, lemon
drops screwed in our ears.
Taking shots down the discharge line,
glancing set-ups, speaking
in flashlight.
Came in high, then
almost flat.

Water coming up as we leave
in clown-suit waders, ducking on the back
of a low,
yellow train.
Icy streams down the neck. Blue
circle at the end,
the weather has lifted into sunlight.

Back in camp, Irishmen sing
in the ventilator, stack the walls with beer,
shore up the ceiling.
No one drives
in their own dreams. Amid bears,
the pastry cook pans
for nuggets in the clattering river.

KIZHUYAK BAY

The tanner crabs (the kings
have disappeared) we hoist up
(with a drowning tan cod) in the trap
of strong, blue netting,
make crunching sounds,
they want to go back down deep in the water
and scuttle away.
They don't even try.
One of them keeps poking its mouth
anxiously with a small, white, inner claw.
I can see myself, now.

CONSTRUCTION

Work in construction, wages, good
at balancing lumber
on my shoulder, know where
to saw and when not to.
Get up in the morning pouring
coffee, concrete, eat
my lunch at noon,
talk over the job, what
was on last night, jokes like open
scars on the tongue.
Paid by the hour
by hour.
There are benefits, there is
trouble, not only stepping
on a 16d duplex nail some punk left
sticking up for Jesus,
or losing teeth
to a spud wrench, something else
like the weather of how
things are done. Smooth, clear
there's nothing better, scratching
red into blue.
Then, in the evening
you know, my beer, my show, dropping
off in the chair. Weekends.
Car. House.
The family. One Sunday, alone
it's raining
I walk over and look out the window.

AFTER DARK

The Terror Lake hydro-electric project
used a machine, the Mole,
to grind out a tunnel
twelve feet across through granite
or whatever
it came to in the cold, white nerves of the mountains.
Now, from deep in the lake
running the seven miles of this tunnel
a pipe bends down
steeply to the powerhouse
into a triple manifold, into triple turbines
and the toast
pops up in Kodiak, miles away, the light
is steady,
a sizzling form appears, and leftover
signals rise into space
scribbled as songs.

The wires
on their cruciform towers hum, run-off refills
the wind-whipped lake, no fish
dammed, earth
faced with a lot of hard-cured concrete
embedded with steel
backed into boulders, its two
ancient floatplanes sunken into legend,
out of reach,
whose once remote and freezing eye
sees back into our lives
where, filling our pockets
with snow
we stay to the goat-trail ridges, watching
for bear, though we always
come down with the birds and the deer
into the valleys before dark.

LOOKING FOR MARTHA

Using a five power glass
I watch her by the flowers
fade into absoluteness.

Behind her, a small blue window of blue sky
high in the corner
of a tangled green wall of leaves.

She is standing in the Lambert Gardens,
Portland, August, 1963, having never seen
nor heard of me.

The shadow of her face rests
along her neck and shoulder.
Those white flowers

have followed her all this time
they shake the dust from their leaves
and gather around her.

SURFACING

Looks like a nice day
from in here,
through the slats, between
the trees.
Cats are taken in by windows.
Within a week

there'll be rain, adding to the creeks
and rivers, rivers
whose sternwheelers have long since burned,
been looted, turned to muck.
How many cords of wood, stacked
along the banks, would it take to steam from
Whitehorse to La Paz, imagining,
where necessary, blue lines
meandering between us?
Or tons of coal by train, rails
dashed in real time across the map—stopping how often
to take on water?
Long waits, dangling at the borders.

The tracks a different gauge, wider, going into Russia.
Guard against invasion.
The Nazis had to switch
wheels, wheel
undercarriages of trains designed
like suits of quick-change artists.

   Railroads are named
for the cities, the country they cross.
All rivers
have taken many names—each one
will never change, it is
the river.

But it isn't.
The rain is different, in season
it's the same,
having only to fall. Sometimes

it changes rivers.
Anything can happen. Surfacing
in a leaking sub
off the northern coast of Arizona, part
of an invading force…
but we soon surrender
to the mild weather
and go home
where rain will change to snow, drift
above the windows…

    But not today, a day held wide and blue
in her golden eye,

    for the moment.

YESTERDAY WAS WALT WHITMAN'S BIRTHDAY

Riding my blue American bicycle
along the river, the brown-braided, rain
eating Chena, someone
I seem to know,
going my way, waves from their rented rubber canoe
drifting through a slow curve.

Glancing back, I'm still passing the river,
coasting by the pond
where the city takes snow from its streets,
Silurian marsh, guarded by unlovable brush
and rusty barrels, sail
beneath the bridge, shift gears
onto Peger Road,
standing on pedals.

There is an instant, slicing
through a wide, silver puddle of Interior,
North Star Borough rainwater edged
with the brittle, receding afternoon
teeth of morning ice, in which
I see how fast and far we go, held up
on skinny tires
by a moment of force,

balanced in the distance,
on the water.

THE RIGHT WORDS

I'd rather stay home
looking for the right words, combing
old typewriter ribbons through a glass.
Pretty soon, I begin to think
I've gone beyond white shirts hanging
under my elevated bed,
where I do my dreams and my dreams, me.
Why get things straight,
it's all a flash
in the brain pan anyway.
The shavings in my transparent pencil
sharpener will start
a fire someday, the smoke will rise
saying everything I did, or tried.
An old Indian, holding down the earth
under his crossed legs,
will say, "How pleasant…" But the real
meaning, in his language—he's the last
one who speaks it—
will be lost in the sky's.

BATTLEFIELDS HIT BY A RAINSTORM

Twist in the wind,
sizzling bolts of white fire, huge drums, one drop,
then another, then all
at once smacking the earth like bullets
hitting a corpse. All morning
it won't let up
and pours into afternoon, the sharp light
cracking, deadening drums in the black cauldron of clouds.
Then, near evening, with a final surge of power
that nails the wind
down on the yellow mud,
it stops
as though someone had signaled,
cutting at their throat with the back of a finger.
Clouds begin to break
apart, and the cool sun has only time to shrug
before sinking into a pool of glowing red
that drains off into the distant,
saw-tooth mountains, and is soaked away
in snow. Overnight

the fields bloom, color
after color,
and by midmorning, under the new, hot sun
bees are waltzing in their doorways,
the birds are wild with singing,
and in a nest, hidden in tall grass growing greener
and greener at the edge of the fields,
are eggs
of the bluest sky.
Around one, a crack is forming.
Something dark and wet moves inside,
quivers, and the crack grows wider, showing the white
inner shell. Wider, slowly
exploding. At noon
the sun sees itself again
and again
in the hellholes of rainwater.

LOWER CAMP

Two
snowmen
drunk by the
mess hall
their eyes
lost
after a hard
rain
among all
the other
shiny
black
shiny pebbles

LOST

Mirrors, windows still
waters: either too quick and sharp
or the world
peers over my shoulder.
I'm superimposed.
I'd never be on tv, even turned off,
plug pulled
from the wall:
I might be someone else,
or no one at all.

Since it's not for an answer, slick
as a lie, only
what's there, under changing, a feeling
of going inside,
I'll look for myself
in your eyes—
not those twin dolls of myself,
tiny as insects,
whose minuscule gestures flail
at the atoms of sense,
but my own

eyes following the thread
of your vision leading inside
you, mixed by your heart
into your mind,
then seen in your eyes
mixed into mine…
Ah, I'm lost in this way.
Without you I'm blind.

RED HANDED AT THIRTY BELOW

Not thinking,
bitter night, so I leave
it running—
And when I return in a minute, cold
milk in my arms,
it is gone.
I run up and down, it's
none of the others:
nothing is there
—oily space—
where it idled,
a dream
full of warm, blowing air.
I try to rise, fly

up over the labyrinth
of icy streets,
the roads out of town.
But I stay on the ground,
stuck to my feet.
Slowly aware,
now,
of my life.

III.

AWAKE

Selecting a spoon from the drawer,
I stir my coffee.
The morning sky is milk.

Somewhere,
like a lost dream, a tiny knot
in the chemistry—

how the surgeon,
emerging faceless from the mist in long,
tight gloves, took

his vivid knife to me—opened wide.
Sleep dripped down
through a vein, and then, since

hearing is the hardest sense to deaden,
I listened. His voice
changed at what he saw inside.

The first thing I remember
being held by someone
outside a peeling, blue trailer house

in a field of tall, dry weeds. Not
knowing what to see,
seeing everything.

DECOY

Looking across the concrete-
block fence, open shapes
of four-leaf clovers mortared in its face,
seeing the top of a palm tree:
this could be Mexico.
Or is it?
Looking for birds to tell me.
The shrubbery won't.
Neither will the flowers,
nor the sky half-muffled with clouds
where a hawk,
in a higher wind, crosses
fast without moving a wing. Sprawled
on my back, unblinking
stare, will it circle
down thinking I'm dead.
Is it true? A child
I practiced death hard, machine guns
pecking my heart:
I let in darkness as long as I could
in such a strong light.
Somewhere,
I look down on my body.
The hawk sails over the border.

THE DEEPS OF HAPPINESS

In those days you went down breathing
in a bucket,
maybe
ten feet.
Now it's a lung
strapped to your back—the deeper
you go, the less
you can spend,
writing your name on slates,
descending. Until
it's no longer a name
in the world, let alone
yours. And a fine
champagne uncorks in your blood,
down becomes up.
Enraptured, you offer
air to the first friendly face
of a fish. Smiling
in your glass
mask you forget
how to breathe,
you're so happy.

THIRD GRADE

By a stack of lumber-ends,
our play blocks, holding
a piece of 2x4, sawn-
off in a flannel shirt, fat cheeks, looking
at the camera, is that me? No
reason in my eyes.
Outside the one-room school, classmates,
some at a tilting table,
were there so few?
The Indian kneeling across from me,
isn't that Jimmy who lived
in an old cabin with his grandfather
who'd been a rodeo rider?
Bill and Norman, and their sister, Mary
three grades ahead,
standing tall to her smile!
Looking back,
the little I can, squinting,
turning sideways,
to what I felt then: someone
so small, seen now
like a fallen-in star
suddenly burst into fire.

BY THE POOL

The sun at your neck,
you lounge by the pool, its orange
tube tethered to a vagrant

breeze, while above,
the sky eats a distant, blue engine.
Down at the deep end

an old crocodile, glass jaws,
a broken-off leg,
sleeps on the bottom, guarding

the drain.
Even crippled
and dead to the world, he flickers

with teeth and a thrashing green tail-
diving in, holding
a quick prayer in your hands.

BECAUSE THE DRUM

Stopped in my tracks,
the flies in heaven, birds
try out for paradise.
Wide open arms,
my shirt on the line
welcomes the sun.
A little dog
barks at the future. A door slams,
a car drives away—flowers
and trees,
the flowering trees. Gone
by or going
to be going, no time's
like the present
to the sky.
Even the doctor, tapping
my hollow insides,
plays a note of forgiveness.

MORTALITY TABLES

He dreads dying in the supermarket,
tomatoes rolling in the aisle, as in a dream
groping at some final displacement of pain,
searching deep in his pockets
for the fire of oxygen.
But who wants to know when the random static
of death will enter the stethoscope.
It could be with no revelation,
in spite of green tongues in the leaves
and hydrangea
igniting the houses,

a way of escape, leaving everyone else to their
vague sense of tint, as brushed on windows
streaked with raindust, this freedom
unseen before now, rising up
at his feet.
He said three years were too long
and not long enough. The strenuous pleasure
of running the rapids, the growing loss of appetite,
closing hours, and church.
A week, a day,

the adventure of knowing, or not,
except in the crystal
of mortality tables fogged by his breathing.
Any minute then, about ten on a Saturday morning,
the sun burning an earlier haze
from the mountains. He stands, barefoot
on the warm floor, looking
from the window at the plumes of white smoke
that thin out and vanish,
leaving the blue sky, as always
alone and untouched.

YOUR NAME IN WHITE

At the crossing, boxcars following a long whistle
stop the future
both ways, change to round,
black tanks full of lemonade and margaritas.
On one, Rodriguez
sails by, scrawled large in white spray.
    From the caboose's upper window
a languid brakeman cools
an elbow—
the rhythms, like weak stations
in the mountains, fade, wheels
melt into measured rails—Time begins
again in first:
the barriers lift and lights and bells
withdraw into their shells.

Rodriguez combs his thick, black hair
once between his fingers,
raps up and peels away.
    Rodriguez, as into the wind,
begins to speak,
and saves our lives.

OVERLOOKING THE AIRPORT

A white butterfly shows
in flashes
above the low, rock fence. Inside,
mangoes ripen by the sink.
Last night, a wind
picked up in the mind, sang
in the struts—
The streets are still wet.
Mynahs nest in the bedroom wall,
red bits of plastic,
cellophane, blue eggs and all.
Small doves, feeding low
to the earth,
rarely fly.

I'll be right back.

SONNET TO A MORE TROPICAL
SATURDAY AFTERNOON

Heart swims, waking sea
water in my ear—four
little girls, noise-
makers in their spokes, ride
the streets, coast
the slanted drive
of an empty house. Birds
in latticework shade
in neighboring cages, sing
among themselves—

Nor are the others, two on a wild branch
of bougainvilleas,
quiet on the cadences
of Haydn.

TO THE EAST

In my sister's flowery yard, the sky
is going to seed.
The sun fills bottles with purple light,
turn-of-the-century elixirs, vials
for opium the Chinese
inhaled away forever when they cleared
the fields of rocks
that rose into boundary walls.

And the mock orange tree
that charmed me with its splendid fruit,
thick skinned, hollowed out
unnecessary hearts—ornaments
to be spat out.
How my nephew's friend, the neighbor
in its sour shade
must dream of Viet Nam. We missed the wars,

my father and I, too young
or too late. And then he is gone
before the last,
wanting to see how things would happen.
And maybe he did, in broken light,
like flying the ox-armed Sacramento
to the wide Pacific fields
that touch another sky.

AXLE

Rounding a blind
curve in India, the axle of an oxcart
he cannot avoid rips open
the side of his Volkswagen bus
laden with wine and tuna fish
from Nuremberg, soft cheese
and cigars.
From the back of the cart
a corpse springs up from its flowers,
rolls in the ditch.
    A moment the silence of bones
hangs in the dust.
He'll come back a fly, or a man
with no eyes.
A starving hole opens in his face.
He steps down
hard, gives it the gas.

TROUBLE

There are problems along the road,
a bad noise in the engine.
The radio still plays
its own brand of music, the news like smoke
in the distance,
and new diets.
Someone will stop—the hood is up—
and give us a hand.

They zip by, like we were,
racers to the same cold fire.

FROM A TRUE STORY

The little girl who plays the part
has better teeth
and doesn't die, but the white
make-up on her face
like cake
might well see her off into old age.
As a young woman tossing
in the hot starlight
of her sky
it will glow in her forehead
like the shadow of an angel.
Her lovely children, collecting money
for their teeth,
will have it too—their X-rays
snapped into the viewer.
A doctor, who plays a doctor, sighs,
uses up our eyes.

STREAMLINER

Delayed in stations, it seems forever
on our separate ways, your train is leaving,
beginning to move,
is moving, its green windows drifting
past, each car
rocking to sleep
on the wavering rails, gaining momentum,
the clicking wheels…

Pure luck, a glimpse
of your face lost amid the blazing
reflections of this summer day, where I'm confused
in glass, each dim passenger
becoming one of me,
my image on a strip of film, blurred
until the train,
its thousand windows annealed

into one, vanishes
across the shimmering fields. And who is left
to ride the world that rattles
in its wake, the trees
swept back, the flying grass, scattered towns
and bridges of resonant steel
carried off behind that sorrowful
and distant engine.

JET

Through the dragon
breathing dark a jetliner blinks.
Second-class angels.
In the seatbacks no Bibles, but magazines
of golfing vacations; diagram
with arrows showing exits,
how the mask will drop down:
you first, then the child.
Some fly their dreams
of tiny, white pillows, others
talking, laughing, cheeks
full of ice.
From here, on the earth, a light
growing dim,
bringing miles behind
the ghost-roar of its engines.

RIVERTRIP

Sweepers are trees fallen out
in the river
to catch your happy canoe
coming out of a corner.
Isn't that it?
In a swift current, too late
to avoid…
All your things float away,
or sink,
leaving you
in a tree with a paddle.

THE REAL WEATHER

The earliest part, like the lost
ox, may be gone over
the horizon,
but according to the big, green trees,
the light in their leaves,
it's still morning
and wires running the town do not
yet hold us together.
Now, and then, the good tube draws dust.

Apart from those of getting in
and out of cars
with bad brakes, there's a channel devoted
to the weather:
someone standing in their shoes
sweeps an open hand across the bordered country
marked off in codes
of meandering color—golden
hot spots, like melting butter, grey
drizzle of an Irish hurricane.
A satellite picture,
live, shows the sky we look up
to. Imagine, our real faces, ourselves
down there, between the clouds,
if we blew it up, not having
to guess.

ONE MORNING

Crusts of toast on a plate, blue
vines twining
and twisting around its lip.
Where are my socks?
Here they are.
Now, where are my feet? Oh, yes
she is singing.
Sunshine eggs, grated potatoes,
and cowboy coffee.
I wear a red shirt.
A stranger's broken my broom:
yellow handle, red
thread running through the straw.
In two, sweeping
snow from his face. Snap:
buttons of pearl.

REFUSE

The garbage men come
in a truck
so noisy it's orange,
so loud it's Friday. Empty
the galvanized
cans, remove
the black bags from our lives,
an act we
depend on, pay taxes—
Stuff we can't use, bones
& old food, dust
from the vacuum,
the news. Maybe
in the blue moon of today
they'll find something good:
a radio works,
music flies out.
This heart is not broken!

IT MOVES, SOON IT WILL FLY

In one of the chambers, like sockets
in the skull of a small creature
whose face lacked everything
but eyes, of the nest
mud-daubed above our heads on the front porch,
grows the hornet of God.
As yet, neither wings nor eyes.
The body is grey, weak legs
enfolded. Hunger
comes before the jaw; the sting
is beginning to sharpen. It moves,
soon it will fly, alight
on still waters and drink.
It will eat of obsessions, moths
fattened on light
and be alive—yellow and black. Like love
pinched off into venom.

TERMINAL

A jar on a bench
painted green, green
painted head of a nail protruding,

is empty, of glass.
Beside the jar, in its broken
light, a lid,

turned up.
Without the lid on its mouth
the jar can breathe…..

but the lid
has a duty to stop, to trap
the emptiness,

hold it tight before all the nails get out,
abandon their unpainted holes
to be eaten by rust.

MEDICINE

Do I need what I'm looking for?
Do we ever tune in on the same dream,
waiting at a station
looking down a road built up between fields?
Can one see things far away, medicine
in a cabinet even the pharmacist
is unaware of?
Will the traffic get so dense
no light can escape?
My father said he wanted to live to see
what would happen.
Do all the horizons finally come together?
How do you feel?
And me.
Why is it so hard to tell.

THE SPRING OF '87

The news from my mother,
murder, snow
in Red Bluff.

READY OR NOT

Maybe like my father,
when his leg ran away without him.
Cousin Charlie, catching, holding it down
until it stopped.
Then my father laid out on his bed,
very still, his eyes
held in by the ceiling
before he is ready…

THIN CLOUDS

rise from a teacup
By the cracks in my teeth
a bad winter

Gripping its stick my one-
legged heart, stalks
the room: Door, Table,

Stove, No gold in the floorboards
only coins from China
square holes in their centers

I could have walked there
and back
The moon drifting

on that shallow mountain
named for me
Gone when I get there

SOMEDAY

Looking ahead, my face is not so clear.
Don't we see in a certain light
we feel we're shining?
It's in my eyes.
Someday I have to die—Just keep it off
the calendar. For all I say,
there are wheels,
and there are wheels for prayer.

Shading my eyes, the features
are like a sketch in the papers:
someone glimpsed at the scene by moonlight.
Eyebrows a little higher.
The mouth, neutral.
But I was always here at the time,
It isn't me.
Is that what I'm afraid of?

. You can't be anywhere at once.

WHERE

What else is there to say
to say, the world
goes wild, wild
the cities stretch out their arms in smoke,
the fields of dust.
My mind goes
back to where its never been, in me
at least,
trailing my skin behind it
like a robe.

THE GAMBLERS

The last time I came home
is with the gamblers. Late, everything closed.
Inviting each other
into the kitchen, they do a little step,
loosen things up—
and the whole visible world flies out
through their fingers.

The dice
like double-locomotives
cast out across a desert's frozen rivers...
and they never stop
rolling long enough, rounding corners,
to think they know the true,
magnetic north, their streaks

of winning, losing.
Out shoot the Jesus cards
from a frayed collar, greased ace from a threaded
sleeve. They bring me home,
but not to sleep
or drowse in any skeletal chair—I have
to spend, turn

my pockets into innocence, down to copper
my grandmother saved, she,
holy roller, long gone,
singing to another shore. Snap! youth
drawn to the inside straight, they
bring me home, spinning out, teeth laced with dark,
gold beer, laughing

into the closed-off eyes above the low
hanging light, spreading their hands, one
suit into the next, jack

elbowing the king,
deuce
saving, without thought, the seven, one
at a time, the odds

clicking off. The diamonds laid out,
and clubs, rolling
snake-eyes, polished bones
of smoke saved from all the fires made
of clashing stones. Before
the cards go soft, lose their riffle, now

at the kindling fire, awakening
the heart's queen, face
down on thin veneer. The last time
I came home
is with the gamblers, wild
as the one-eyed, flying through their arms out
into air,

sail into their upturned hats.

ABOUT THE AUTHOR

Jerry Cable grew up on a ranch in Fall River Mills, a small town in the northeastern corner of California. He served in the Army in the early 1960s, and after discharge, earned a BA from Chico State in 1965. In 1967, looking for adventure, he flew with a pilot friend in a small plane from San Francisco to Fairbanks, Alaska. Over the next 20 years, he worked as a surveyor, built a cabin with his partner, and made a close community of friends. All this time he wrote: radio plays, journals, and poetry. In 1982 he earned an MFA in poetry from the University of Alaska, Fairbanks. He continued working seasonally as a surveyor, always capturing his world in poems. In 1987 he was diagnosed with cancer and left Fairbanks to pursue treatment. He spent the last months of his life in Red Bluff, California awake to all around him, writing his life this last time in his poems. He died in Chico, California early in 1988.

ABOUT CIRQUE PRESS

Cirque Press grew out of *Cirque*, a literary journal that publishes the works of writers and artists from the North Pacific Rim, a region that reaches north from Oregon to the Yukon Territory, south through Alaska to Hawaii, and west to the Russian Far East.

Cirque Press is a partnership of Sandra Kleven, publisher, and Michael Burwell, editor. Ten years ago, we recognized that works of talented writers in the region were going unpublished, and the Press was launched to bring those works to fruition. We publish fiction, nonfiction, and poetry, and we seek to produce art that provides a deeper understanding about the region and its cultures. The writing of our authors is significant, personal, and strong.

Sandra Kleven – Michael Burwell, publishers and editors
www.cirquejournal.com

BOOKS FROM CIRQUE PRESS

Apportioning the Light by Karen Tschannen (2018)

The Lure of Impermanence by Carey Taylor (2018)

Echolocation by Kristin Berger (2018)

Like Painted Kites & Collected Works by Clifton Bates (2019)

Athabaskan Fractal: Poems of the Far North by Karla Linn Merrifield (2019)

Holy Ghost Town by Tim Sherry (2019)

Drunk on Love: Twelve Stories to Savor Responsibly by Kerry Dean Feldman (2019)

Wide Open Eyes: Surfacing from Vietnam by Paul Kirk Haeder (2020)

Silty Water People by Vivian Faith Prescott (2020)

Life Revised by Leah Stenson (2020)

Oasis Earth: Planet in Peril by Rick Steiner (2020)

The Way to Gaamaak Cove by Doug Pope (2020)

Loggers Don't Make Love by Dave Rowan (2020)

The Dream That Is Childhood by Sandra Wassilie (2020)

Seward Soundboard by Sean Ulman (2020)

The Fox Boy by Gretchen Brinck (2021)

Lily Is Leaving: Poems by Leslie Ann Fried (2021)

One Headlight by Matt Caprioli (2021)

November Reconsidered by Marc Janssen (2021)

Callie Comes of Age by Dale Champlin (2021)

Someday I'll Miss This Place Too by Dan Branch (2021)

Out There In The Out There by Jerry McDonnell (2021)

Fish the Dead Water Hard by Eric Heyne (2021)

Salt & Roses by Buffy McKay (2022)

Growing Older In This Place: A Life in Alaska's Rainforest by Margo Wasserman Waring (2022)

Kettle Dance: A Big Sky Murder by Kerry Dean Feldman (2022)

Nothing Got Broke by Larry F. Slonaker (2022)

On the Beach: Poems 2016-2021 by Alan Weltzien (2022)

Sky Changes on the Kuskokwim by Clifton Bates (2022)

Transplanted By Birgit Lennertz Sarrimanolis (2022)

Between Promise and Sadness by Joanne Townsend (2022)

Yosemite Dawning by Shauna Potocky (2022)

The Woman Within by Tami Phelps and Kerry Dean Feldman (2023)

In the Winter of the Orange Snow by Diane S. Carpenter (2023)

Mail Order Nurse by Sue Lium (2023)

All in Due Time by Kate Troll (2023)

Infinite Meditations For Inspiration and Daily Practice by Scott Hanson (2023)

Getting Home from Here by Anne Ward-Masterson (2023)

Crossing the Burnside Bridge & Other Poems by Janice D. Rubin (2023)

A Variable Sense of Things by Ron McFarland (2023)

Tiny's Stories: An Athabascan Family on the Yukon River
    by Theresa "Tiny" Demientieff Devlin with Sam Demientieff (2024)

If Singing Went On by Gerald Cable (2024)

May the Owl Call Again: A Return to Poet John Meade Haines, 1924-2011
    by Rachel Epstein (2024)

Out of the Dark: A Memoir by Marian Elliott (2024)

CIRCLES

Illustrated books from Cirque Press

Baby Abe: A Lullaby for Lincoln by Ann Chandonnet (2021)

Miss Tami, Is Today Tomorrow? by Tami Phelps (2021)

Miss Bebe Goes to America by Lynda Humphrey (2022)

MORE PRAISE FOR *IF SINGING WENT ON*

Reading Gerald Cable's posthumous book *If Singing Went On* is like listening to an intelligent friend telling you about his day. He reels out thoughtful descriptions with insight and fresh metaphor from an active and capacious mind. Ranging from observations of abandoned dredges in Alaska to harvesting the garden in fall "…the cold heart of joy." He surprises at every turn… Against the hard metal of industry, he flashes forth with organic metaphors connected to the natural world… He would have us know, as he says to a friend, "It's cold, Emily, and the world sails hard for the sun." His words come to us alive as ever.

— David McElroy, author of the poetry books *Just Between Us* and *Water The Rocks Make*

www.ingramcontent.com/pod-product-compliance
Lightning Source LLC
Chambersburg PA
CBHW020941090426
42736CB00010B/1219